A Dog for a Friend

To my own little girls, Natalie and Maureen,
who settled for a hamster and a budgie.
M.R.

For Paula and Katie
who gave Jessie her smile.
S.M.

For Naomi — a future teacher!
Marilyn Reynolds

ORCA BOOK PUBLISHERS

A Dog for a Friend

Written by MARILYNN REYNOLDS
Illustrated by STEPHEN McCALLUM

Many years ago, before you were born, a little girl named Jessie lived with her mother and father on a farm a long way from anywhere. Great fields of wheat stretched out on all sides of the farm and there were no other people for miles around.

There were few radios or telephones or cars or trucks or airplanes. The world was quiet when Jessie was a little girl, and often she was lonely. More than anything, Jessie wanted a dog for a friend.

Jessie tagged along behind her mother and father as they planted the seeds, harvested the grain and cared for the animals.

"Can I have a dog?" she asked her mother one day.

Mother held up the shirt she was washing, frowned and dropped it back into the washtub. She wiped her wet forehead against her arm. "There's far too much work around here for me to even think about getting a dog," she said. "Hand me that bar of soap. And bring me a pail of water off the stove." Mother plunged her red hands back into the suds.

On another day, as Mother carried the heavy pails of water from the well, Jessie tried again. "I'd be good to my dog and I'd feed it every day," she promised.

Mother set the pails on the ground and paused to rest. "If we raised cattle or sheep, we'd have a dog to help herd the animals. But this is a wheat farm. We don't need a dog." Then Mother smiled. "Maybe we'll get one someday."

Jessie crouched in the black dirt and helped Mother pull carrots from the garden. "A dog would be my friend," she said quietly.

At this, Mother stopped. She straightened up to ease her aching back. Cleaning her hands on her apron, she rubbed a smudge of dirt off Jessie's face. "I don't know if any of the neighbours' dogs have a litter of puppies," she said. "We won't be going into town for a long time, but when we do, we'll ask around. If there's a puppy available, we'll talk about it then. You'll just have to wait. Why don't you ask your father about it sometime?"

Father sat on a stool in the hay-scented barn milking th
cow.

"Can I have a dog?" Jessie asked.

"A dog?" Father stopped milking. "Why would you want
dog when we have all these cats? Cats are good at catching
the rats in the barn. A dog isn't the best rat catcher.
Besides," he teased, "we don't need a sheep dog or a cattle
dog on a wheat farm, do we?"

"A cat won't come when you call it," explained Jessie. "A
dog would always come. A dog would play with me. He'd
fetch a stick and I could teach him to roll over and beg for
his dinner. And he'd sleep with his head on my lap."

Father looked at Jessie. "I know what you can do," he
said at last. "If you gather the eggs every morning and if you
help us with the pigs, I'm sure Mother will see that you can
take care of a dog yourself. Now, let's feed those cats!"

Turning on his stool, Father shot streams of milk into the
cats' waiting mouths. When they were full, the animals crept
into the dark corners under the eaves to wash their dripping
faces. Father stood up. "Help me carry the milk to the house.
One of these days I'll talk to your mother about getting you
a dog."

But as time went by, Mother was always too busy mending socks or canning fruit or making butter to listen. "Someday you can have a dog," she said, "but right now I have too much to do without worrying about a pet. Perhaps we'll find one when we go to town next time."

Early every morning, Jessie shooed the hens off their nests in the straw and gathered their eggs, thinking all the while how good it would be to have a dog beside her. She imagined how her dog would look, and she drew pictures of dogs in her scribbler.

When she helped Mother in the kitchen, she thought of all the games she would play with her dog.

Then one autumn afternoon, the old sow in the barn had her litter. One little piglet was smaller, thinner and weaker than all the others. The other piglets nursed hungrily, but there wasn't room for the littlest pig to eat. And later, when the other babies slept like a row of pink sausages next to their mother's side, the littlest pig couldn't fight his way to a warm place. "Look at the smallest one. He's left all by himself and he's crying," Jessie said to Father.

She spent the next day peering through the slats of the pen. "That pig's not getting enough to eat," she told her parents at supper.

Father frowned. "I'll look in on him in the morning," he said.

By the following day, the runt was too weak to fight for a place to nurse. He lay by himself in the hay. "Can't we bring him into the house?" Jessie pleaded. "I promise I'll look after him."

So that evening, when the first frost of the season dusted the garden, Father carried the tiny piglet into the kitchen. "I guess we're going to have to save this runt," he said.

Jessie found a wooden box and made a bed in it with a suit of Father's worn-out long underwear. She set the box beside the woodstove where it was warm. Mother got out an eye dropper, and everyone took turns feeding the piglet warmed milk. When bedtime came, Jessie tucked the runt into his bed and kissed him goodnight on the top of his head.

"That's enough," said Mother, laughing. "It's getting late and we've spent enough time on that pig."

Father blew out the lamp and they all went to bed. For a little while everything was quiet.

Then, alone in the darkness and the silence, the baby pig began to cry. His cries started as whimpers and grew into sobs that sounded just like a human baby's. They filled the house until Jessie couldn't stand it any longer.

She jumped out of bed and ran to the kitchen. "He's crying," she called to her parents as she picked up the piglet and held him tenderly against her chest.

"Put that pig back. He'll stop when he gets tired," Father called back.

"Go to bed!" added Mother.

"Can't I take him to sleep with me?" Jessie begged.

"Don't be silly," said Mother.

Jessie reluctantly laid the pig in his box beside the stove and went back to her room. Before she climbed into bed, the piglet started crying again. Jessie wondered if the baby was longing for his mother and brothers and sisters. She lay in her narrow cot with eyes wide open, listening.

It must be nice, she thought, to lie in the hay next to your mother and sleep with your brothers and sisters, all warm and cozy. No wonder the piglet doesn't like sleeping by himself.

As she lay thinking, Jessie realized that the crying had suddenly stopped. She strained to hear, but there was no sound coming from the kitchen.

He must have fallen asleep, she thought. She listened intently, but all she could hear was the ticking of the clock on the wall, the soft hoot of a barn owl and the wind in the grass outside her window. She closed her eyes and was almost asleep when a terrible thought struck. Maybe the pig had hurt himself.

Maybe something had happened to him.

Anxiously, Jessie tiptoed back to the kitchen in her nightgown and bare feet. The little bed beside the stove was empty. There was no piglet to be seen. She looked all around the floor in the moonlight, under the woodstove, behind the woodbox, around the kitchen table and in every corner.

Jessie ran up to her parents' room. "The pig's gone! He's not anywhere," she cried.

She stopped at the doorway. Father had fallen asleep and was snoring softly on his side of the bed, but Mother was awake, and a strange, smooth lump lay beside her shoulder. Jessie tiptoed closer. Snuggled up against Mother's arm with the blanket tucked up to his chin, the little piglet was sleeping happily.

Mother's face grew red. "Get back to bed," she whispered. She tried to frown, but her eyes crinkled and her mouth curled up into an embarrassed smile.

Mother shrugged. "He sounded so unhappy that I thought I'd bring him here – for just a minute." She looked at Jessie's surprised face and began to chuckle. "I knew he was missing his mother," she said sheepishly.

Mother slowly sat up in bed. Gently, she picked up the runt and laid him in Jessie's hands. "Don't wake him," she said as she leaned forward and gave Jessie a big hug.

Jessie took the sleeping piglet and carried him back to her own bed. I'm going to call him Harold, she thought as she laid his head on her pillow.

As the days passed, Harold got bigger and stronger and noisier. He was a very intelligent pig. He knew his name and he always came when Jessie called him. He followed her around the kitchen and he learned to fetch a stick and roll a ball with his flat, quivering nose. And sometimes he slept with his head on Jessie's lap.

When he grew too big to sleep in his box by the kitchen stove, Harold went back to live with his brothers and sisters in the barn where he ate more slops than all the others.

One day in the spring, Mother arrived home from a neighbour's farm with a tiny puppy in the pocket of her coat. Jessie finally got the dog she'd always wanted.

And Harold, who had been so small and so helpless, grew to be the biggest pig for miles around. He won first prize at all the fairs, and he became the father of hundreds of other pigs who looked exactly like he did.

Publication assistance provided by The Canada Council.

Orca Book Publishers
PO Box 5626, Stn B
Victoria, BC V8R 6S4
Canada

Orca Book Publishers
#3028, 1574 Gulf Road
Point Roberts, WA 98281
USA

Canadian Cataloguing in Publication Data
Reynolds, Marilynn, 1940-
A dog for a friend
ISBN 1-55143-020-7 (pbk.)
I. McCallum, Stephen, 1960-   II. Title.
PS8585.E973D63 1994   jC813'.54   C94-910364-0
PZ10.3.R49Do 1994
Printed and bound in Hong Kong
Design by Christine Toller
10 9 8 7 6 5 4 3 2 1